Who Cloned the President?

by Ron Roy
illustrated by Liza Woodruff

SCHOLASTIC INC.

New York Toronto London Auckland Sydney
Mexico City New Delhi Hong Kong Buenos Aires

Dedicated to kids who love books
—R.R.

To Carolyn
—L.W.

ISBN 0-439-68447-1

12 11 10 9 8 7 6 5 4 3 2   4 5 6 7 8 9/0

Printed in the U.S.A.   40

First Scholastic printing, September 2004

Contents

1
KC's Discovery

KC Corcoran pulled a slip of paper out of her teacher's baseball cap. She read the words on the paper and grinned.

"Who did you get, KC?" Mr. Alubicki asked.

"President Thornton," KC said.

"No fair!" Marshall Li protested. "You already know everything about him."

Mr. Alubicki smiled and passed the hat to Marshall, KC's best friend. Marshall picked a slip. "Herbert Hoover?" he said. "I don't even know who he is!"

"But you'll know all about him after you write your report," his teacher said.

Mr. Alubicki finished passing the hat around the room. "Okay, everyone, have a great weekend. Get started on your president reports. We'll discuss them Monday."

KC grabbed her backpack and followed Marshall out the door. They walked home together every day.

KC and Marshall lived in the same ten-story building in Washington, D.C. It stood between a pet shop and a Chinese restaurant.

They stopped on the way home to watch puppies and kittens through the pet-shop window.

"Why is everyone so crazy about furry animals?" Marshall asked. "Spiders make great pets, too!"

KC laughed. "Marsh, you can't cuddle up with a spider."

"Who says you can't?" Marshall asked. "I wish Mr. A. would let us write about insects instead of presidents."

Marshall loved anything with more than four legs. He kept jars of crawly things in his bedroom. Spike, his pet tarantula, slept in one of Marsh's old baseball caps.

"Presidents' Day is in February," KC reminded her friend. "If we had an insects' day, Mr. A. would let you write about Spike."

"Spike's not an insect," Marshall said. "Tarantulas are spiders, and spiders are arachnids."

"I know, I know," KC said as she pushed open the glass door of their building. "You've told me a hundred times!"

"And you still don't remember," grumbled Marshall. He pushed the elevator button.

Donald, the building manager, opened the elevator door. Donald ran the elevator and helped people get taxis out front.

"Hi, kids," Donald said. "Got plans for the weekend?"

"We have to write reports," Marshall told him. "About dead presidents."

"Mine's not dead," KC told Donald. "I picked President Thornton!"

Donald smiled as he pressed the button for Marshall's floor. "Lucky you! Maybe you'll see him around town."

Marshall got off on the third floor, and Donald took KC to the fifth. She let herself into the apartment with her key.

Lost and Found, her two kittens, came skidding across the wood floor when the door opened. KC rubbed their bellies, then headed for the kitchen.

A note was taped to the fridge.

KC—I'll be home around six. Have a snack. Love, Mom.

KC grabbed a banana and walked into the living room. Lost and Found scurried after her. She pulled *Your Presidents* from a bookshelf and looked up President Thornton.

"Listen," she said to the kittens. "Zachary Thornton had five brothers and sisters. He raised chickens and sold eggs to help his family." Then the caption of a picture caught her eye. "As a Boy Scout, Zachary Thornton earned twelve merit badges," she read.

"See, Marshall was wrong," KC mumbled. "I don't know everything about

President Thornton. I had no idea he got twelve badges in Scouts."

KC marked the page, then switched on her mom's computer. She logged on to the Internet and found more about President Thornton. "Zachary Thornton is our fourth left-handed president," KC read.

"Cool. We're both left-handed!" KC said. She kept reading and noticed a headline from *The Washington Post* newspaper. "President Thornton Says No to Human Cloning."

KC read the rest of the paragraph about scientists cloning animals. Marshall had told her that some scientists wanted to clone humans.

"I'm glad the president said no," she said. "I only want one of me!"

KC shut off the computer and turned

on the TV. She flopped on the sofa and pulled the kittens onto her lap.

Cindy Sparks, the White House reporter, was just signing off.

"Someday that'll be me," KC told her kittens. She planned to become a TV anchorwoman after college.

KC peeled the banana and channel surfed. She found a live special on President Thornton at a press conference in the White House.

"Tomorrow morning," said President Thornton, "I will make an announcement that will change human life forever."

Then someone handed the president a stack of papers. He signed them slowly, as if he were tired. He didn't smile or talk to anyone around him. He just took a paper, signed it, and reached for another.

Hmmm, thought KC. *It's not like him to be so quiet and serious. He looks sick.*

KC noticed something else. "That's weird," she said. She called Marshall and told him to turn on channel 3.

"It's the president," Marshall said a few seconds later. "So?"

"Do you see anything weird?"

"Like what?"

"Marsh, he's signing those papers with his right hand!"

Marshall laughed. "You called to tell me the president is right-handed?"

"No, he's *left*-handed!"

"Oooh, let's call 911," Marshall said.

KC kept staring at the president on TV. Signing with the wrong hand. Looking tired and way too serious. Almost like a different person. . . .

Her imagination kicked in. What if this guy was a fake? What if the real president had been kidnapped? What if he'd been drugged or . . . KC shook her head.

She could almost hear her mom warning her—for the millionth time—not to jump to conclusions.

Then she remembered that headline: "President Thornton Says No to Human Cloning."

"That's it!" KC cried.

"Marshall, get up here right now!" she yelled into the phone. "Someone cloned the president!"

2
The Plan

A few minutes later, KC's doorbell rang. She let Marshall in.

"All right," he said. He threw himself onto the sofa. "Tell me why you think the president has been cloned."

KC sat in the chair by Marshall. "You don't believe me? Look!" On the TV, President Thornton continued to sign papers. "He's signing papers with his right hand!"

Marshall stared at KC. "That means he was cloned? Maybe he hurt his left hand."

"There's other stuff, Marsh," KC said. She pointed to the TV just as the president stood up. He walked away without saying a word. "Don't you think that's weird?" asked KC. "He didn't smile or shake hands or anything. He acts like I did when I had the flu!"

"So, maybe he has the flu."

KC glared at Marshall. "Having the flu wouldn't make him sign papers with his other hand!" she said. "Something is wrong with him!"

Marshall glanced at the TV screen. The president was gone. Reporters were packing up to leave. "He did look a little different," Marshall admitted.

"He looked different because it wasn't him!" KC said. "It was a clone!"

Marshall stared at KC for a minute. "Okay," he finally said. "Let's say you're right. The President of the United States has been cloned. Who did it? Why? When?"

KC paced back and forth in front of the sofa. "I don't know! Don't try to confuse me," she said. "But that guy on TV didn't act the way our president acts. I know, Marshall. I watch him every night!" KC kept pacing.

"You're making me dizzy," Marshall said.

"Shhh, I'm thinking," KC said. She stopped pacing. "Got it!"

Marshall slumped into the sofa pillows. "I don't think I want to hear this," he muttered.

"Listen, I'll tell my mom I'm sleeping at your apartment tonight. You tell your parents you're sleeping here."

"Why?"

KC shoved him toward the door. "I'll tell you later. Meet me downstairs in five minutes!"

"But wh—?"

"And bring a jar of your spiders!"

Before Marshall could say another word, KC slammed the door. Grinning, she ran to the kitchen. She wrote a note for her mom, then grabbed some snacks from the fridge.

She charged into her bedroom and dumped the school stuff out of her backpack. She tossed in the snacks, a flashlight, her Swiss Army knife, and a tape recorder. At the last minute, she opened her bank and took out a fistful of money.

She grabbed a jacket, said good-bye to her kittens, then let herself out of the apartment.

Donald opened the elevator door. "Going out again, KC?"

"Me and Marshall are doing some research for our reports," she said.

It's not a total lie, thought KC. She paced as she waited for Marshall in the lobby.

When he showed up with his backpack, KC dragged him outside.

"Did you bring the spiders?" she asked, heading toward the bus stop.

"Yeah, but where are we going?"

"To help the president. He needs us."

Marshall stopped walking. "KC, I've known you practically my whole life. But you're acting weird. Why does the president need two fourth graders?"

The number 6 bus stopped. KC dropped quarters into the box, then pulled Marshall into a seat.

"I'm waiting," Marshall said.

KC glanced around her. The bus was nearly empty.

"Okay, I think the guy on TV was a fake or a clone," KC whispered. "If he is, what happened to the real president?"

Before Marshall could open his mouth, KC went on. "Marshall, the president is in danger! And we're going to save him!"

Marshall shook his head. "I'm in my bed. I'm having a terrible nightmare."

KC opened her eyes innocently. "All I want to do is help my country!"

Marshall stared glumly out the window. "Another question," he said. "We both lied about where we're sleeping tonight. So, where are we really sleeping?"

KC grinned. "In the White House."

3
Spider Surprise

The bus dropped them a short walk away from the White House.

KC looked at her watch. "That must be the last tour of the day. Let's get in line."

Since it was February, there weren't many tourists. KC grabbed Marshall's arm and joined the group.

"KC, can I ask a dumb question?" he whispered. "Why am I sneaking a jar of spiders into the White House?"

KC whispered her plan.

"Now I know you're nuts!" he hissed. "We're not going to sleep in the White House. We're going to sleep in jail!"

KC shushed him. "Just remember to throw the spiders when I give you the signal," she whispered.

"But how will I get them back?" Marshall asked. "I raised these spiders from babies! They love me!"

"Marshall, just think. Your spiders are going to save the President of the United States," KC said. "They'll be famous! Charlotte only saved a pig!"

"Charlotte who?"

KC raised her eyebrows.

"Oh," Marshall said, looking embarrassed. "*That* Charlotte. Anyway, what's your signal?"

KC thought for a moment. "Neck. When I say neck, you toss the spiders."

"Neck? How're you gonna work 'neck' into a conversation?"

"Trust me. Just be ready, okay?"

The line moved. Pretty soon KC and Marshall were inside the White House.

A woman in a blue suit met the group. "Good afternoon, everyone. My name is Debbie. I'll be your guide today. And since Lincoln's birthday was last week, we have opened the Lincoln bedroom for all tours!"

"Will we see President Thornton?" someone asked.

Debbie smiled. "I know he's in the building. Keep your eyes peeled."

Marshall smiled for the first time in an hour. "Maybe I can get the president's autograph!" he said.

In the Lincoln bedroom, the guide pointed out the paintings and antique furniture. "In Lincoln's term, this was not a bedroom. So he never slept in this magnificent bed," Debbie told the crowd.

The tourists said "oooh" a lot and asked questions.

"Open the jar," KC whispered.

Marshall stared at her. "Here? Now?"

She nodded. "Move away from me. Mix in with the crowd." She pointed to her neck. "And get ready for you-know-what!"

With a sick look on his face, Marshall went to stand behind three nuns. KC watched him stick both hands inside his backpack.

"If there are no more questions," the guide said, "we can move on to—"

"I have a question," KC said. She waved her arm like she did in school.

"Yes?" Debbie asked.

Everyone turned to look at KC. Suddenly she screamed, "SOMETHING IS ON MY *NECK!*"

She began jumping and slapping at her neck. "MY NECK! SOMETHING IS CRAWLING ON MY NECK!"

Out of the corner of her eye, she saw Marshall toss the spiders. No one else noticed. They were all staring at KC.

Then a woman screamed. "SPIDERS! THERE ARE SPIDERS IN MY HAIR!"

"Ugh!" the guide yelled. She swiped at a black spider crawling on her arm.

Suddenly there seemed to be spiders everywhere. Two dozen tourists panicked at once.

Everyone ran out of the room, screaming and slapping at their bodies.

With an unhappy look on his face,

Marshall slipped the empty jar into his backpack.

KC looked around. They were alone. She grabbed Marshall and dragged him down under the Lincoln bed.

"It worked!" KC whispered.

"And we're fourth-grade felons!" hissed Marshall. "Plus, I lost all my spiders!"

"Your spiders will be heroes," KC said.

"But we'll be prisoners," Marshall sputtered. "Why do I listen to you?"

"Because I'm your best friend," KC said, calmly opening her backpack.

"Juice?" she asked.

4
Under the Bed

KC drank her apple juice and ate raisin cookies. Marshall curled into a ball and glared at her.

"Aren't you hungry?" KC asked.

No answer.

"Are you really mad at me?"

Marshall closed his eyes.

"Okay, but there are only two more cookies!"

Marshall reached out a hand. "*If* we ever get out of here," he said, "I *might* forgive you."

They finished the rest of the snacks in silence.

KC kept checking her watch. Marshall sighed a lot and looked for his spiders. He didn't see any.

KC curled up and took a nap.

Marshall scratched at a mosquito bite on his ankle.

Hours later, a clock bonged ten times.

"Finally!" KC said. "Okay, Marsh, it's ten o'clock. Let's go." She crawled out from under the bed.

Marshall was right behind her. "Go where?" he asked, stretching his back.

The Lincoln bedroom was dark. Only a small light was on, near one of the doors.

"To rescue the president," KC said. She smiled at her best friend. "Maybe you will get that autograph," she added.

Marshall snorted. "I bet he's brushing his teeth and getting ready for bed." He slung his backpack over his shoulder. "Like we're supposed to be doing!"

KC smiled. "And the real president brushes his teeth with his left hand!"

She opened the door and peeked into the hall. Like the bedroom, it was nearly dark. Small lights shone on the portraits hanging on the walls. Vases of flowers stood on polished tables.

"Come on," KC whispered over her shoulder. She yanked on the first door knob they came to. It was locked. "Try every door," she ordered.

Just then a man in a uniform came around a corner. Luckily, he was looking at the floor, not straight ahead.

"Guard!" KC hissed. She grabbed Marshall and hurried him through a small door. It led to a set of stairs.

"Let's go down here," KC whispered.

"I need to find a bathroom," Marshall said.

KC whipped around. "Why didn't you go at home?"

"I did, but that was a long time ago. We were under that dumb bed for about a year! And besides," he added, "breaking into the White House always makes me a little nervous!"

KC started down the stairs. "Maybe there's a bathroom down here."

A few minutes later, they found themselves in a huge, dark kitchen. KC twisted a dimmer switch on the wall.

"Cool!" she said. "This must be where they cook those big state dinners!"

Marshall spied a small door. "I'm gonna see if that's a bathroom," he said.

KC looked around while she waited. The kitchen was in a basement. The floors were tiled. Instead of fancy wallpaper, the walls were painted white.

Marshall came back while KC was twirling a combination lock on an enormous freezer.

"Why do they lock everything in this place?" she muttered.

"To keep people like you out," Marshall grumbled.

They found a corridor and tried more doors.

"I'm getting tired of this," Marshall said. "Can we—"

"Shhh! I hear something!" KC whispered.

They froze and listened. Then Marshall heard it, too.

Somewhere, someone was laughing!

They tiptoed down the passageway, following the noise. Over their heads, pipes ran along the ceiling. Small lights shone down, casting shadows on the concrete floor.

"Look!" KC pointed to a partly opened door.

She heard someone laugh again. Squeezing Marshall's arm, she crept closer and peered around the door.

Then she nearly fainted.

President Zachary Thornton was slumped in a chair, just a few feet away!

5

Two Presidents

KC tugged Marshall into a dark corner. "It's him! He's in there!" she hissed.

"Who?" Marshall hissed right back.

"The president!" she whispered. "With a bunch of other guys!"

KC peeked into the room again. This time she noticed the president's eyes. They looked weird, like they did when she saw him on TV. She backed away from the door and grabbed Marshall's arm.

"Marsh, that's not the president in there. It's the clone!"

Marshall peeked into the room. "I hate to admit it, but I think you're right,"

Marshall said. "He looks like a zombie!"

"What are they doing?" KC asked.

"The clone is in pajamas and a robe," Marshall reported. "Three other guys are with him. They're smoking cigars and watching 'I Love Lucy.'"

Marshall backed away from the door. "Okay, we found the clone. Now what?"

KC opened her backpack and pulled out her tape recorder. She tiptoed back to the door. She clicked on the tape recorder. A deep voice was talking.

"We pulled it off, fellas. Everyone thinks our guy is really the president!"

Other voices joined in.

"—make millions of dollars!"

"—can't wait to see the headlines when we spring our little plan!"

KC hoped the recorder was picking up

every word. The hum of the tape told her she was getting something, at least.

She stared at the president's clone. He was slumped in a chair, wearing slippers, red pajamas, and a blue bathrobe. His eyes looked cold and dead.

Two men in dark suits sat at the table. On it were paper and pens, a small TV, and a few cans of soda. The third man stood by the clone. He was dressed in a white coat, the kind doctors wear.

Suddenly a rough hand grabbed KC by the arm. She turned around. A guard was glaring down at her. The guard's other hand was clamped on Marshall's shoulder.

"March, you two," the guard said. He shoved KC and Marshall into the room.

The three men looked up. The clone didn't budge.

"Well, what have we here?" the man in the doctor suit said. Moving like an eel, he crossed the room.

"I found 'em in the hall," the guard said, "playin' peek-a-boo outside the door!" The guard's breath smelled like sweaty sneakers. His fingers felt like iron on the back of KC's neck.

"Explain yourselves, please," the man in white said. His voice bubbled like he was under water.

"We were on a tour and got lost," KC said.

The man laughed. "A tour at ten-thirty? In the White House basement? I don't think so."

KC had never seen a scarier face. His head was totally bald. Pale blue eyes bugged out, and his teeth were yellow.

His arm shot out. "I'll just have that recorder, please."

"No you won't!" KC said. "I need it for a school report."

The man grabbed the recorder out of her hands. He pushed the REWIND button, then pressed PLAY. Everyone in the room heard the men's voices.

The man in white glared at KC. "Quite the little liar, aren't you?" he said.

"I'm not ly—"

"It's all my fault," Marshall said. "See, we were on a tour, then I decided to go look for the president." Marshall smiled innocently at the glaring men. "I wanted the president's autograph, so I talked my friend into helping me look for him."

Marshall turned to the clone. "Hi, Mr. President. Can I have your autograph?"

The clone didn't even blink.

"The brat's lying through his teeth!" one of the other men barked.

"We'll get the truth later," the man in white said. "For now, they can join our friend. Bring them to the storage room."

"May I please have my tape recorder?" KC asked. "I really need it for school."

The man in the white coat showed his yellow teeth. Then he threw the machine to the floor. When it hit, the tape ejected.

Still grinning, the man ground the tape and recorder under his foot. Soon they were nothing but mashed bits of plastic.

All the men laughed.

"Take these brats away," the man in the lab coat snapped at the guard.

The guard dragged KC and Marshall back into the dark hallway. They both struggled, but the man was too strong.

KC yelled. No one came to help.

"Shut up or you'll be sorry!" the guard snapped.

"You're the one who'll be sorry," said Marshall. "My dad is a lawyer!"

"Big deal," the man growled. "My old man's a bank robber!"

Halfway down the hall, the guard unlocked a door. He shoved Marshall and KC into a dark room.

The door slammed behind them. KC heard the lock turn.

"Are you okay?" Marshall said.

KC couldn't see him. The room was pitch-black. "Yeah, I'm all right," she said, rubbing the back of her neck. "How about you?"

"I'm okay, but what's that smell?"

Marshall asked. "It's like my dad's after-shave lotion."

"Shh, I hear something!" KC said.

Marshall leaned against her in the dark. "Don't say that. I'm scared enough!"

They both stood and listened, holding on to each other.

"Hello," a voice said from out of the darkness.

"Aaahhh!" Marshall yelled. "Someone's in here with us!"

KC dug for her flashlight and switched it on. The beam shone on a tired-looking, familiar face.

"It's okay, Marsh," KC said. "We just found President Thornton."

6
Locked In

The president blinked at the light. He looked tired. The skin under his eyes was saggy, as if he needed sleep. He was wearing a rumpled blue suit and a red tie.

"Who . . . what do you want?" he asked.

KC told the president how she had figured out that he'd been cloned, and about her plan to rescue him.

The president stared at KC. "Cloned?" he asked, rubbing the stubble on his chin.

"Did they drug you, sir?" KC asked. "Is that why you don't remember?"

The president nodded slowly. "Yes, I must have been drugged."

"By those goons who caught us?" Marshall added.

"I—I guess," the president agreed. "I can't remember."

KC shone the flashlight around the room. There was a small bed, a chair, and a radio on a table. On one side was a tiny bathroom.

"Mr. President, your clone is making an important announcement tomorrow," she said. "He's going to tell the world that it's okay to clone humans."

The president didn't say anything. *He must be exhausted,* thought KC.

"We have to stop them!" she went on. "Otherwise—"

"Otherwise those guys will run the world!" Marshall interrupted.

"Yes, stop them," the president said.

KC flashed her light on the door. "First we have to get out of here," she said.

Marshall tried the handle. "Good luck. The door's locked from the outside."

KC examined the door hinges. "Hand me my knife," she said to Marshall. He dug it out of her backpack.

KC opened the screwdriver part of her knife. She began removing the hinge screws. She stood on a chair to reach the top ones.

There were two hinges with four screws in each. It took KC five minutes, but finally she handed Marshall the last screw. "Done," she said.

KC and Marshall removed the door and leaned it against the wall.

KC peeked around the corner. The corridor was dark and empty. "Let's go."

"Shouldn't we put this door back?" Marshall asked. "What if some guard sees it off the hinges like this?"

KC and Marshall managed to set the door in its opening and replace the hinge screws. They left the door closed.

With the president walking between them, KC and Marshall tiptoed back down the hall. They stopped outside the door where the kids had gotten caught.

"The light's still on," KC whispered.

The room was quiet. When KC peeked around the door, she jumped.

The other men were gone, but the clone was still sitting in his chair. Now he was wide awake and tied with thick rope. His mouth was covered with tape. He was struggling to get free.

"We've got to get out of here," KC said.

She thought fast. "Could you come to my apartment?" she asked the president. "You can sleep in the guest room. My mom voted for you!"

The president looked around uneasily. "Yes, let's go."

"Wait! I sat under a bed for six hours for this." Marshall picked up a paper and pen off the table. "Mr. President, may I have your autograph?"

"Marshall!" KC groaned. "We're trying to escape here!"

But the president had already taken the pen and scrawled his signature.

Marshall beamed.

KC nearly fainted.

He had signed with his right hand!

7
Rescued

"Hey, thanks, Mr. President!" Marshall folded the paper and put it in his pocket.

KC stared at the president. Now she didn't know who was the president and who was the clone! If she helped the wrong one, who knew what would happen?

Feeling panicky, KC studied the two look-alikes. The man in the blue suit was right-handed. But KC knew the real president was left-handed.

"What's wrong, KC?" Marshall said. "You look like you swallowed a spider."

KC shook her head. "No, but I just thought of something." She smiled up at the president. "Sir, I need you to go back to the other room."

"Why?" the president asked. He looked confused.

"To buy us some time," she explained. "If anyone looks in, they'll know you're not there. But if you stuff pillows under the covers, they'll think you're in bed."

The president hesitated, then said, "Good idea. I'll be right back."

KC watched him leave the room. When he was gone, she grabbed Marshall. "Follow him!" she whispered. "As soon as he goes into that room, lock the door!"

Marshall's mouth fell open. "Huh? But why, KC?"

"Because he's the clone!" Then she pointed to the man tied in the chair. "This is the real president!"

The man in the chair mumbled behind his gag, nodding his head furiously.

"Now go!" KC shoved Marshall out the door. Marshall gave KC a look, but he hurried down the dark hall.

KC gently removed the tape from the struggling man's mouth.

"Water!" he gasped.

KC looked around the room. There was no water, but she grabbed a can of soda and held it to the man's lips.

After he took a few gulps, KC put the can down. Even in his pajamas and robe, this man looked exactly like the president.

But so did the other one! If she was wrong, she was making a terrible mistake!

Then KC had an idea. "How did you earn money to help your family?"

"I sold eggs to our neighbors," he said.

"How many brothers and sisters do you have?"

The man grinned. "There's Patricia, Trudy, Tommy, Roger, and the baby is Edward. That makes five!"

Anyone might know that, KC realized. "How many merit badges did you earn in the Scouts?" she asked.

The man blinked. "That was a long time ago. Ummm . . . twelve, why?"

Just then Marshall rushed back into the room. "He's locked in," he said. "I hope you're right about which one is which."

"Marshall, don't worry. This is the real President Thornton," KC said, grinning.

"Excuse me," the president said. "But could you untie me?"

"Oops, sorry, sir!" KC took out her knife and cut the ropes.

"Thanks!" The president stood up and rubbed his hands and ankles. "I expected the FBI or CIA, but you two look a little young for agents," he said. "Who are you? And what are you doing in the White House in the middle of the night?"

KC and Marshall introduced themselves and explained again.

The president laughed. "My mother always told me that being left-handed would make me stand out!"

Marshall pulled the folded paper out of his pocket. He looked at the clone's signature, then ripped it to pieces.

He picked up another piece of paper.

"Sir, could I please have your autograph?" he asked the real president.

"Sure, but can it wait? We need to get out of here." He glanced around the room.

"KC, did I hear you say something about your mother's apartment? Could we go there?"

KC nodded. "Won't Mom be surprised when she sees who I brought home!"

The president led KC and Marshall down the corridor. His slippers flip-flopped on the hard floor. He took them back to the kitchen, and stopped in front of the freezer.

"We're going into a freezer?" Marshall said.

The president smiled. "This one is special," he said. He twirled the combination lock a few times. The door popped open.

Suddenly KC heard voices.

"Sir, someone's coming!" she hissed to the president.

8
Secret Passageway

The president pulled KC and Marshall into the cold freezer.

"Hide!" he said as the door closed. He unscrewed a light bulb on the ceiling, then disappeared into the shadows.

Marshall jumped behind a stack of hamburger boxes. KC clambered over the boxes and crouched next to him.

The door to the freezer opened. Light fell onto the floor, and KC saw two shadows appear.

"Hey, Blinky," a man's voice said. "Someone left the lock open. Now's our chance to pig out!"

The two shadows came closer. Horror-struck, KC realized she could see her breath. She clapped both hands over her nose and mouth. Next to her, Marshall did the same.

One of the men stopped only inches from KC. She saw a pair of legs and dark leather shoes.

KC dared to look up from behind the boxes. The man standing there had been in the room with that awful guy in the white coat.

"Nah, it's all vegetables and meat," the man said. "No good stuff."

The feet turned and left. The door shut behind them. KC began to breathe again.

The president stepped out from behind some hanging beef. "Marshall, KC? Are you okay?" he asked.

"J-just a little c-cold," Marshall said.

"Come on," President Thornton said, walking to the rear of the chamber.

At the end of the freezer, the president shoved aside a few sides of beef. Behind them was a blank metal wall. Then the president said, "Zachary Thornton," in a clear voice. KC heard a whirring sound, and the wall slid sideways. In its place was a door.

The president punched in a code on the keypad by the door. The door opened. The kids followed him into a dark tunnel.

"This is so cool!" KC said.

"This secret passageway was built a long time ago," the president explained. "I think Teddy Roosevelt used it once."

"Where does it go?" Marshall asked, peering down the dim tunnel.

"You'll see, but let's hurry," the president said.

The tunnel sloped downhill for a while, then up. At the end, they climbed stairs leading to a door.

This one had a steel bar locking it from the inside. The president slid the bar out of its brackets. Behind the bar was a hole. The president reached into the hole and pulled out a tube.

"Periscope," he said, putting his eye to the tube. After a moment, he said, "All clear. Let's go!"

When the president pulled the door open, KC saw streetlights and cars whizzing by. "We're on Pennsylvania Avenue!" she said.

"That's right," the president said. "Just outside the White House fence."

They stepped through a narrow door onto grass. KC looked back. The door was hidden in a hollow concrete pillar that supported the gate to the White House grounds. When the president closed the door again, it disappeared.

"We can walk to my apartment," KC said. "It's not that far."

The president shook his head. "No, a taxi would be faster. I'm not exactly dressed for walking in February!"

He stepped to the curb, put two fingers into his mouth, and whistled loudly.

A taxi appeared and slowed down. The driver took one look, then sped away.

The president laughed. "I must look pretty strange," he said. His next whistle brought another cab. This one stopped.

"Where to?" the cabby said as the three

climbed into the backseat. She didn't seem to care about the man in his bathrobe and slippers.

"Five hundred 3rd Street," KC said.

"Got it!" The cabby pulled away with a squeal of tires. She looked in the rearview mirror. "Anyone ever tell you you look just like the president?" she asked. "You could be his clone!"

KC looked at Marshall and President Thornton. They all burst out laughing.

"What?" said the cabby. "What's so funny?"

Ten minutes later, the cab pulled up in front of KC and Marshall's building.

The president reached for his wallet. "Oops." His face turned red. "I forgot that I'm in my pajamas. Sorry, but I—I don't have any money on me."

KC rattled the money in her pack. "I do!" She counted out the fare and gave the driver a tip.

"Have a great night!" the cabdriver said before she zoomed away.

Marshall rang the bell on their building. A sleepy-eyed, yawning Donald came to the door. He woke right up when he saw KC and Marshall standing in the street.

Donald opened the door and let the three in. "What are you kids doing out at midnight?"

"Research for our reports," KC said, heading for the elevators.

"Oh, by the way," she added over her shoulder. "This is the president."

9

Slumber Party

"We're all going to my floor," KC told Donald in the elevator.

Donald stared at the president as the elevator rose. The president grinned and whistled "Yankee Doodle." Marshall yawned and scratched his mosquito bite.

At the fifth floor, they all got out. "Good night, Donald," the president said.

Donald beamed. "Good night, Mr. President, your highness!"

KC used her key to let them into the apartment. Her mother was lying on the sofa reading a book.

"Katherine Christine, what are you

doing here?" she said. "I thought you were at Marshall's."

Then she noticed Marshall. "Why aren't you in bed? What's going on?"

And then KC's mom saw the man in the red pajamas and blue bathrobe.

"Mom, I'd like you to meet the president," KC said. "Mr. President, this is my mom, Lois Corcoran."

The president made a little bow. "Delighted, Ms. Corcoran. I owe my life to your daughter and Marshall."

KC's mother stood and removed her reading glasses. She stared at the man in front of her.

He was in his night clothes. He needed a shave. But he was smiling, the way he smiled in his posters.

"Oh my goodness!" KC's mother said,

looking down at her outfit. "I'm in my bathrobe!"

The president held out his hand. "So am I," he said. "So we're even."

KC scooted Lost and Found off a chair. "I hope you aren't allergic to cats," she said to the president.

"I love 'em," he said. "I have a cat in the White House for company." Then he looked at KC's mother. "May I use the phone? I need to alert the CIA that we have some scoundrels in the White House."

"You can use the one in the kitchen," KC's mom said, pointing the way.

While the president was gone, KC told her mother the whole story.

"Spiders?" KC's mom asked.

"Well, it worked," KC said.

"You really released spiders in the

Lincoln bedroom?" her mother said as the president walked back into the room.

Marshall looked up at the president. "Will I get in trouble?"

The president laughed. "Not at all! You two and those spiders are heroes!"

"How did it happen?" KC asked the president. "I mean, how did you get cloned?"

The president pulled up a chair. "It was a very clever plan, actually," he said. "A scientist named Dr. Jenks figured out a way to clone humans. He and his greedy friends spent years perfecting the process. They learned how to make an adult clone from a hair sample. That's what they did with me."

Lost and Found jumped into the president's lap. They began purring.

The president continued. "When my clone was ready, Dr. Jenks set up a meeting to discuss his cloning ideas. I listened to what he had to say, but I told him I was against the cloning of humans."

The president shook his head. "We were having coffee. It was late. My staff had gone home. The last thing I remember is Dr. Jenks saying good night and shaking my hand."

He looked at his listeners. "He must have drugged my coffee and ordered the clone to give the real guards the night off. That was yesterday. I woke up this morning in the basement dressed like this."

"They must have given your suit to the clone," KC said. "You looked drugged when Marsh and I first saw you."

The president nodded. "The drug wore

off, but I pretended I was still asleep so I could listen. With me out of the way, the clone could lie to the world and announce the new cloning policy. Dr. Jenks and his team would make millions cloning humans!"

"But that would be awful!" Marshall cried. "We have to stop them!"

"Don't worry, Marshall," the president said. "The CIA is on the case."

While the president chatted with her mom, KC closed her eyes and dozed off in her chair. She dreamed about Cindy Sparks announcing the news tomorrow:

Local fourth-grade heroes rescue President Thornton and save the world!

10
Spiders Rule

KC peeked out the window in the Oval Office. "Look, Marsh, I see Mr. Alubicki! He's in the fourth row with our class! And there's my mom and your parents!"

Marshall joined her at the window. "Our whole school is out there! Cool!"

It was a week later. KC and Marshall had received A's for their reports. To Marshall's surprise, President Hoover had collected bugs when he was a kid!

But the big surprise was the phone call from the president's secretary. KC and Marshall were invited to the White House. They were going to receive a special award for rescuing the president!

The door opened, and the president walked in. He was carrying two small jewelry boxes. "We'll be going out to the lawn in a few minutes," he said. "But first, I wanted to thank you two in private."

KC blushed.

Marshall noticed a spider crawling down a wall. "Hey, I wonder if that's one of mine!" he said.

The president smiled. "Could be. But don't worry, it'll be safe here. I've issued a memo to all staff. Starting now, spiders are special guests in the White House."

The president handed Marshall and KC each a box. "Please open them," he said.

KC lifted the fancy lid. On a layer of red velvet, she found a satin ribbon and a round gold medal.

"It's beautiful!" she said.

"This is real g-gold!" Marshall cried.

"Read what's inscribed on the medals," the president said.

KC read hers. In a circle were the words: *To KC Corcoran for Bravery.* She flipped her medal over. On the back was an engraving of a spider.

"This is so cool!" Marshall said, hanging his medal around his neck.

"I have one, too." The president unbuttoned his suit jacket and held up his medal. "Mine is just like yours. But it has both your names on the front."

"And a spider on the back?" Marshall asked.

The president grinned at Marshall. "Yep. A spider on the back."

A man peeked in the door. "Mr.

President, they're ready for you outside."

KC gasped when she saw the man's face. "It's the clone!"

The president smiled. "Yes, I interviewed him when Dr. Jenks was arrested. My clone is really a nice guy. He never understood what Dr. Jenks was up to. I've decided to keep him on my staff."

"But won't everyone get confused?" KC asked.

The president winked. "That might be fun," he said. "I've always wanted to have a twin."

He beckoned to the man standing by the door. "By the way," he said to KC and Marshall, "we've given him a special name."

The clone walked over. He proudly showed the kids his name tag. It said, MR. CASEY MARSHALL.

"Wow!" KC said. "We have a clone named after us, Marsh!"

Casey Marshall smiled. "I'll tell them you'll be out in a minute, sir." He left and closed the door behind him.

Marshall dug a paper from his pocket. He held it out to the president.

"You said you'd give me your autograph, Mr. President."

The president took the paper. "You're right, I did promise."

He walked to his desk, picked up a pen, and signed "Zachary Thornton."

With his left hand.

About the Author

Ron Roy is the author of more than fifty books for children, including the bestselling A to Z Mysteries® and the brand-new Capital Mysteries series. He lives in an old farmhouse in Connecticut with his dog, Pal. When he's not writing about his favorite kids in Green Lawn, Connecticut, and Washington, D.C., Ron spends time restoring his house, gardening, and traveling all over the country.

The Capital Mysteries

Read all of KC and Marshall's adventures in Washington, D.C.!

When the President of the United States starts acting funny on TV, KC decides he's not the *real* President Thornton. She's sure he's a clone!

KC's mom and President Thornton have disappeared during the Cherry Blossom Festival. They were kidnapped—right under the bodyguards' noses!

Leonard Fisher claims he's the heir to the Smithsonian fortune. If KC and Marshall can't prove he's a liar, Washington will lose its world-famous museums!

Look for Ron Roy's A to Z Mysteries, too!